THE BEAR UNDER THE STAIRS

D0794673

Helen Cooper

For Ted

THE BEAR UNDER THE STAIRS
A DOUBLEDAY BOOK: 0 385 40210 4
A PICTURE CORGI BOOK: 0 552 52706 8

First published in Great Britain by Doubleday,
a division of Transworld Publishers Ltd

PRINTING HISTORY
Doubleday edition published 1993
Picture Corgi edition published 1994
Reprinted 1994, 1995 (twice), 1996
1997, 1998, 1999

Copyright © 1993 by Helen Cooper

The right of Helen Cooper to be identified as the author of this work
has been asserted in accordance with the Copyright, Designs
and Patents Act 1988

Condition of Sale
This book is sold subject to the condition that it shall not, by way of
trade or otherwise, be lent, resold, hired out or otherwise circulated
without the publisher's prior consent in any form of binding or cover
other than that in which it is published and without a similar condition
including this condition being imposed on the subsequent purchaser

Doubleday and Picture Corgi Books are published by
Transworld Publishers Ltd,
61-63 Uxbridge Road, Ealing, London W5 5SA,
in Australia by Transworld Publishers (Australia) Pty. Ltd,
15-25 Helles Avenue, Moorebank, NSW 2170
and in New Zealand by Transworld Publishers (NZ) Ltd,
3 William Pickering Drive, Albany, Auckland

Made and printed in Belgium by Proost

William was scared of grizzly bears,
and William was scared of the
place under the stairs.

It was all because
one day he thought
he'd seen a bear,
there, under the stairs.

And he'd slammed the
door shut –
wham, bang, thump!

William worried about the bear.
He wondered what it might eat.
'Yum, yum,' the bear said, in William's head.
'I'm a very hungry bear,
perhaps I'll eat boys for tea!'

So William saved a pear for the
bear who lived under the stairs.

And when no-one was watching,
William whipped out his pear,
opened the door,
threw the pear to the bear
that lived under the stairs,
then slammed the door shut –
wham, bang, thump!

William had kept his eyes shut tight,
so he didn't see the bear
in its lair
under the stairs.

But he knew what it looked like!

And at night...

while William dreamed...

William.
by Bear

Every day, William fed
the bear that lived under
the stairs.

He fed it bananas, bacon and bread.

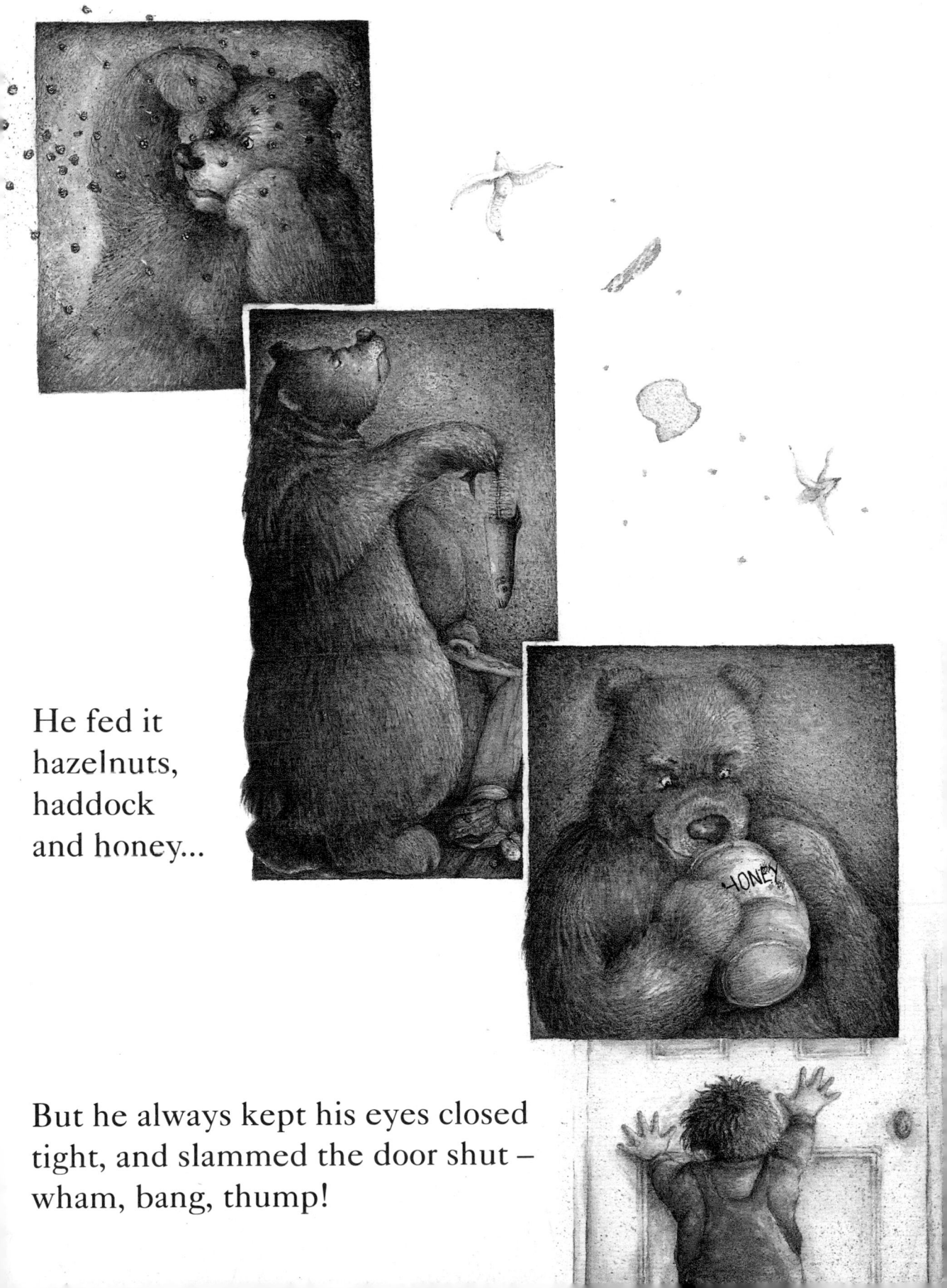

He fed it
hazelnuts,
haddock
and honey...

But he always kept his eyes closed
tight, and slammed the door shut –
wham, bang, thump!

After a while there was a strange smell,
in the air,
near the bear,
under the stairs!

The smell got stronger, and stronger,
until his mum noticed.
'There's an awful pong,' she said.
'I think I'd better do some cleaning.'

‘No!’

screamed William, very scared.

‘Don’t go in there!’

Mum lifted William on to her lap.
'William, whatever's the matter?' she asked.
So William told her all about the hungry bear
in its lair, there, under the stairs.

Then William and Mum went to fight
the bear that lived under the stairs.
Brave William had his eyes wide open
all the time,
and when they opened the door,
he saw...

An old furry rug,
a broken chair,
no bear,
no scare,
and horrible stinky food everywhere!

So William and
Mum cleaned up.

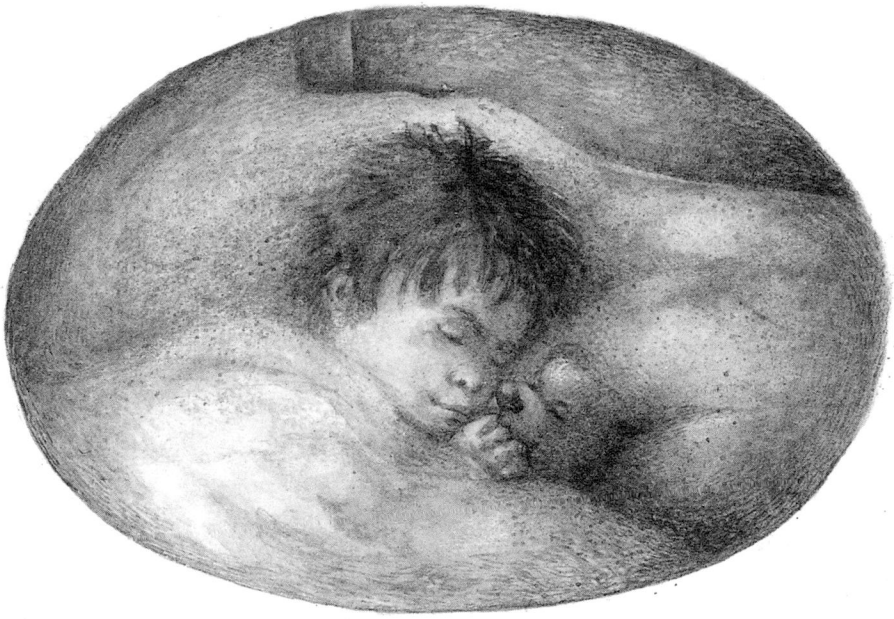

Then they went shopping and
bought William a little brown grizzly
bear of his own. It had such a nice
face that William was never scared of bears ...

Gon

Gone
Away

... ever again...